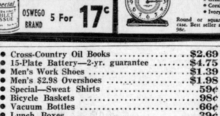

4 Sue ~ J.P.L.
4 Aidan & Olive ~ V.F.

eye M enormously grateful 2 Pat, who was a perfect plum ball-b along the way. eye would like 2 thank Barbara Ensor 4 her invaluable insight, and Mary Sherwood & Jacquie Strasburger 4 their selective scrap scavenging. eye would like 2 thank David, Aidan & Olive 4 their advice & encouragement. eye M exceedingly grateful 2 Rachael Cole 4 her patience & craft, & 2 Anne Schwartz & Lee Wade 4 gleefully shoving me through doors eye hadn't even considered opening. —V.F.

Text copyright © 2010 by J. Patrick Lewis ✳ Illustrations copyright © 2010 by Valorie Fisher ✳ All rights reserved. Published in the United States by Schwartz & Wade Books, an imprint of Random House Children's Books, a division of Random House, Inc., New York. ✳ Schwartz & Wade Books and the colophon are trademarks of Random House, Inc. Visit us on the Web! www.randomhouse.com/kids ✳ Educators and librarians, for a variety of teaching tools, visit us at www.randomhouse.com/teachers

Library of Congress Cataloging-in-Publication Data ✳ Lewis, J. Patrick. ✳ The Fantastic 5 & 10 [cent] store : a rebus adventure / J. Patrick Lewis ; illustrated by Valorie Fisher. – 1st ed. ✳ p. cm. Title contains symbol for "cent." ✳ Summary: Rhymed text, featuring rebuses, describes the wonders of the store run by Mr. Nickel and Mrs. Dime. ISBN 978-0-375-85878-9 (trade) – ISBN 978-0-375-95878-6 (glb) ✳ 1. Rebuses. [1. Stories in rhyme. 2. Stores, Retail–Fiction. 3. Rebuses.] I. Fisher, Valorie, ill. II. Title. III. Title: Fantastic five & 10 [cent] Store. ✳ PZ8.3.L5855Fan 2010 ✳ [E]–dc22 ✳ 2008048827

The text of this book is set in Egizio. ✳ The illustrations are rendered in mixed-media collage. ✳ MANUFACTURED IN CHINA
10 9 8 7 6 5 4 3 2 1
First Edition

The Fantastic 5&10¢ Store

A REBUS ADVENTURE

words by
J. Patrick Lewis

pictures by
Valorie Fisher

schwartz & wade books · new york

The  poured heat on S + T,

Big +s filled with ,

As +flakes +ed in+2 sleet.

The weather was insane!

But what at the end of town

Nobody could X+ .

The  guessed "A of ."

The , "A ?"

"A piece of ," the barber yelled,

"Has fallen from the sk+ !"

And so the guessing GAME went on

Till each 1 had a tr+ .

"Y, it's a ," the said.

"Or else a  !"

"NON+¢+S," replied the , "it's

A GIANT +er drawer!"

Then Ben+ shouted, "That's

The 5&10¢ Store."

The +come hooted once,

So Ben+ raised the latch.

He heard a funny thump-thump-thump,

And then a scritch & scratch .

When Ben+ entered, +s

And were playing +ch.

The *owner*, Mr. , spun

Round & round again.

"We have had a customer

Since Mrs. was 10!"

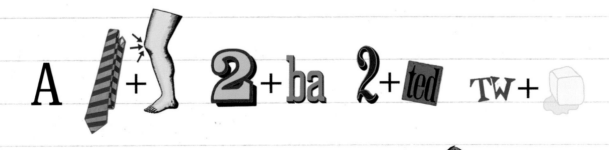

A + 2+ba 2+ted TW+

And scared a *plastic* .

A ![toaster] with ![flamingo] ![wing]+**S**

Flew over, popping ![bread].

A ![paintbrush] dipped itself in green,

![PAINT can]+**ing** the ceiling red.

And 2 ![nails] could ![knot] **W**+**8** **2** hit

A ![hammer] on the ![head].

The  said **2** the saucer, "U

R quite a dish, m+  d+ !"

The calendar *jumped* off the

+cause it was leap y+ ,

 made a

A t+ .

A  and a bottle

From the stand

Had flipped their lids & wobbled 2

The LITTLE Rubber .

Said Mrs. , "And give

The a !"

A  led a deck of .

They marched **in** single file,

And shuffled **2** the  of +S

 the Hardware +L.

The  receiver told

The 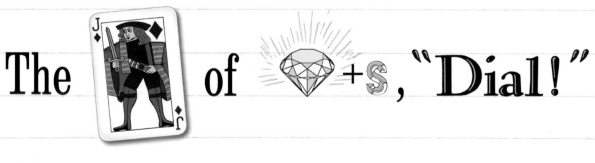 of +S, "Dial!"

Then Mrs. said, "Ben+ , we

Think U R very wise.

Please  the and R+

And C who wins the prize.

We'll count on U, of course, 2

The judge in case of +S."

The 🥘 R + ♠ + ed through the 5&10,

But soon the 🫖 led.

Cheer + 💍 them on, 🎈 and 🚩.

A 🧸 bounced on a 🛏 !

And at the finish 🐟 + ing line,

The 🫖 steamed a + 👤.

The tipping  2+ ted, "Wheee!"

Accepting her award—

A , a , and

A LITTLE  .

"Next R+ , the  twins!"

The napkin holder roared.

Still, Mr. [nickel] [crying] + ed a t+[ear],

And Mrs. [dime] wept 3.

"If only people came 2 shop,

We'd give them prizes, FREE!

Pink [lollipop]+s, blue Hula Hoops–

How *lovely* would that [bee]?"

A 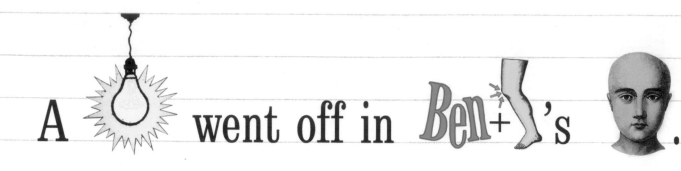 went off in Ben+'s .

"I'll hang some twinkling +s

 customers won't have 2 guess

At who & where U R.

They'll come by and ,

By , and !"

And so they do. The  knocks,

The barber 💍+S the chime,

The 🔪 and the 👨‍🍳, 2.

They STOP in all the time

At the 1&5&10¢ Store—

THE .

... The Fantastic 5 & 10¢ Store ...
A REBUS ADVENTURE WITHOUT THE REBUSES

The sun poured heat on Pumpkin Street,
Big buckets filled with rain,
As snowflakes barreled into sleet.
The weather was insane!
But what rose up at the end of town
Nobody could explain.

The butcher guessed "A leg of lamb."
The baker cried, "A pie?"
"A piece of cloud," the barber yelled,
"Has fallen from the sky!"
And so the guessing game went on
Till each one had a try.

"Why, it's a bus," the mailman said.
"Or else a dinosaur!"
"Nonsense," replied the doctor, "it's
A giant dresser drawer!"
Then Benny Penny shouted, "That's
The 5 & 10 Cent Store."

The welcome owl hooted once,
So Benny raised the latch.
He heard a funny thump-thump-thump,
And then a scritch and scratch.
When Benny Penny entered, cats
And mice were playing catch.

The owner, Mr. Nickel, spun
Round and round again.
"We have not had a customer
Since Mrs. Dime was ten!"
A tiny tuba tooted twice
And scared a plastic hen.

A toaster with flamingo wings
Flew over, popping bread.
A paintbrush dipped itself in green,
Painting the ceiling red.
And two nails could not wait to hit
A hammer on the head.

The cup said to the saucer, "You
Are quite a dish, my dear!"
The calendar jumped off the wall
Because it was leap year,
Which made a crocodile cry
A crocodile tear.

A mustard and a ketchup bottle
From the hot-dog stand
Had flipped their lids and wobbled to
The Little Rubber Band.
Said Mrs. Dime, "And let us give
The pickle jar a hand!"

A Joker led a deck of cards.
They marched in single file,
And shuffled to the Queen of Hearts
Down the Hardware aisle.
The telephone receiver told
The Jack of Diamonds, "Dial!"

Then Mrs. Dime said, "Benny, we
Think you are very wise.
Please watch the Pot and Teapot race
And see who wins the prize.
We'll count on you, of course, to be
The judge in case of ties."

The Pot raced through the 5 & 10,
But soon the Teapot led.
Cheering them on, balloon and flag.
A doll bounced on a bed!
And at the finish fishing line,
The Teapot steamed ahead.

The tipping Teapot tooted, "Wheee!"
Accepting her award—
A baseball cap, a yo-yo, and
A little pirate sword.
"Next race, the Salt & Pepper twins!"
The napkin holder roared.

Still, Mr. Nickel cried a tear,
And Mrs. Dime wept three.
"If only people came to shop,
We'd give them prizes, FREE!
Pink lollipops, blue Hula Hoops—
How lovely would that be?"

A light went off in Benny's head.
"I'll hang some twinkling stars
So customers won't have to guess
At who and where you are.
They'll come by train and tricycle,
By scooter, bus and car!"

And so they do. The doctor knocks,
The barber rings the chime,
The butcher and the baker, too.
They stop in all the time
At the 1 & 5 & 10 Cent Store—
The PennyNickelDime.

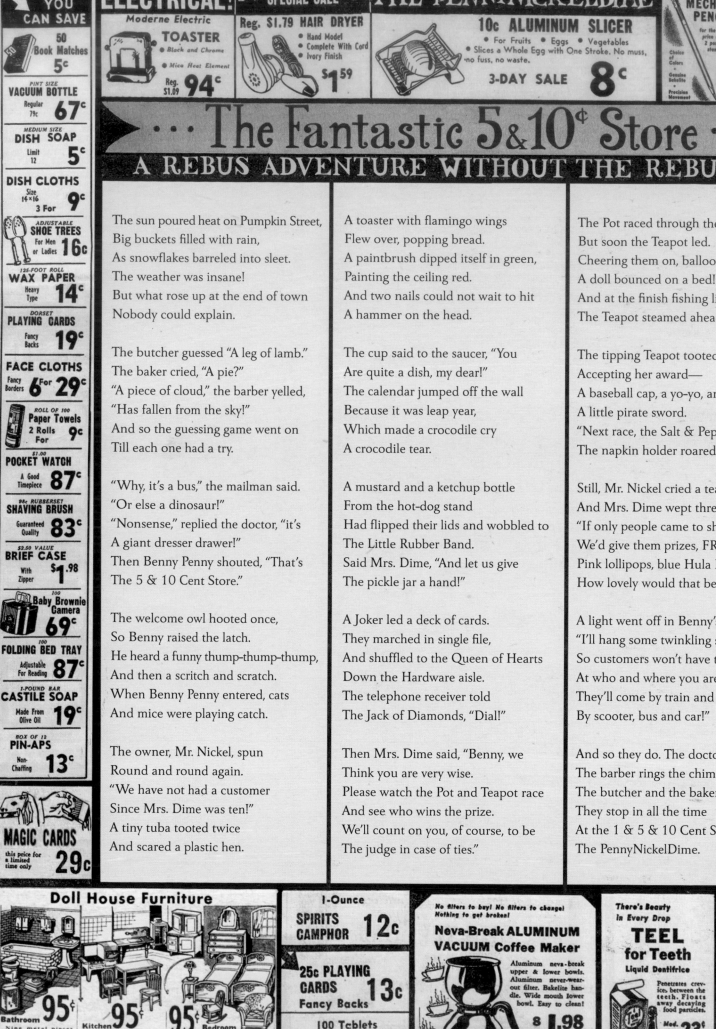